William Kotzwinkle, Glenn Murray and Elizabeth Gundy

Walter the Farting Dog
and the Windy Day

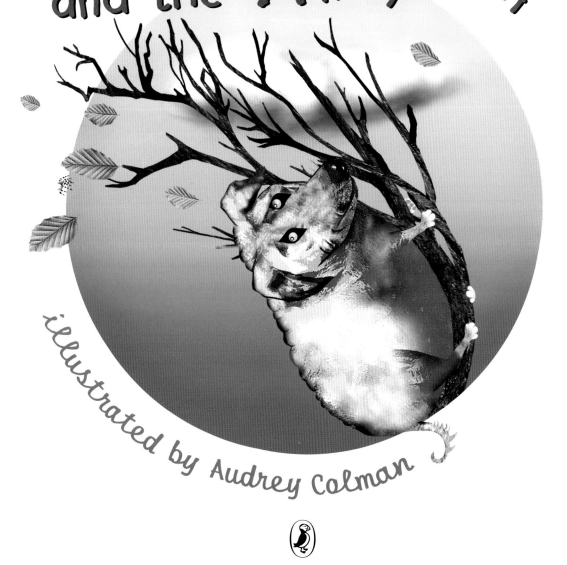

illustrated by Audrey Colman

PUFFIN

PUFFIN BOOKS
Published by the Penguin Group: London, New York, Ireland, Australia, Canada,
India, New Zealand and South Africa
Penguin Books Ltd, Registered Offices: 80 Strand, London WC2R 0RL, England

penguin.com

First published in the United States by Dutton Children's Books 2005
Published in Great Britain in Puffin Books 2006
3 5 7 9 10 8 6 4 2
Text copyright © William Kotzwinkle, Glenn Murray and Elizabeth Gundy, 2005
Illustrations copyright © Audrey Colman, 2005
Manufactured in China
ISBN-13: 978-0-141-50050-8
ISBN-10: 0-141-50050-6

For everyone who's ever felt
misjudged or misunderstood

Professor Kompressor knocked on the door.
"I understand your dog has a farting disorder."
"It's not a disorder," said Betty and Billy.
"Yes, it is!" shouted Father. "Come on in."

Professor Kompressor said, "I've made a lifelong study of animal gas."

He examined Walter, gently poking around his stomach.

"You'd better be careful," said Father. "He farts when you do that."

"He won't fart at me, will you, Walter?"

Walter farted. Professor Kompressor staggered backwards, waving his gas meter. "Ten-point-seven! The highest I've ever recorded. What a remarkable animal."

Walter was pleased to be called remarkable. He liked Professor Kompressor and licked his hand.

"You're a good dog, Walter," said Professor Kompressor, "and I'm going to help you."

He poked around some more. "It's his digestion that causes such powerful farts."

"We don't mind," said Betty and Billy.

"Yes, we do," said Mother.

"Years of research have led me to this special formula," said Professor Kompressor. Powders and potions appeared from his pockets. He plugged in a gleaming machine. "Mix it in my Kompressatron and serve it fresh three times a day."

"We're so grateful," said Mother.

So three times a day Mother mixed the special formula in the Kompressatron.

"His farts aren't as bad," said Billy hopefully.

"They're worse than ever," said Father.

"Your father is right," said Mother.

That night Father decided to mix the formula himself. He examined the powders carefully. "More of *this*," he decided. "Less of *this* and a *lot* more of that."

Father sniffed the new mixture and smiled. "That's better."

Tastes pretty good, said Walter to himself, and ate it faithfully every day.

"It's working!" cried Mother. "The air smells so fresh."

"Hurray!" said Betty.

Walter was pleased, too. Everyone was smiling. No one ran away when he came in the room. Father even hugged him.

However, inside Walter, gas was building up slowly.

"That dog's getting fat," said Father.

But it wasn't fat.

It was farts, waiting to be set free.

Professor Kompressor's mixture and Father's expert touch were turning Walter into a blimp.

Walter began taking strange little bounces when he walked across the room.

One evening he floated over Father's chair.

"Great jump, Walter," said Billy.

But it wasn't a jump. It was gas.

The following evening Billy and Betty were in their room doing homework.

"Billy," said Betty, "look outside!"

Betty and Billy raced out of the house.

Walter was floating over the trees.

"Walter, come down!" cried Betty.

But Walter couldn't come down.

He floated on into town.
Quite a view, he said to himself.

A breeze came up and blew him over to the other end of town.
This is getting serious, said Walter.

He knew the problem was gas. He knew the solution was farting.

He squeezed.

He pressed his belly with his paws.

He twisted into a knot.

Nothing.

He floated all night long. When morning came, he was high above the world.

"Mummy," said a little girl, "look at the balloon."

"It's lost," said the little girl's mother. "It will never come back."

Walter floated for days. He floated over green hills and blue rivers. He floated over skyscrapers and farms. He floated in the dark and the rain.

He felt lonely and cold.

He went whichever way the wind carried him.

Suddenly the wind grew much stronger and he wasn't alone any longer.

The air around him was filled with the flutter of tiny, frozen wings.

Millions of butterflies were caught in a freezing windstorm. They had been on their way to their winter home when the storm took them by surprise.

Poor butterflies, said Walter to himself.

The wind was driving them down towards the frozen lake below.

I've got to help them, thought Walter.

He knew he had it in him, if he could just get it out. He grunted. He groaned. He pressed.

He looked into their tiny insect faces. It was now or never.

He let rip.
A blast of warm gas lifted the butterflies out of their dive.
It melted the ice on their wings. It carried them to the far side
of a mountain, where the sun was shining.

They touched down in a field of wild flowers.
A forest ranger in his tower grabbed his two-way radio.
"I think those butterflies are going to be okay."

Out of gas, Walter went down like a rocket.

He splashed into a pond and doggy-paddled to the shore.

He shook himself dry. Then he sniffed the air, turned round and started the long walk home.

He'd gone only a little way when the ranger pulled up in his Jeep. "Can I give you a lift, Wonder Dog?"

"Somebody has sent us a big package," said Mother, looking out of the window.

"It's not a package!" cried Billy. "It's Walter!"

"See," said Father, "I told you he'd find his way home."

"Oh Walter," said Betty, "we're so glad you're back."

"Not half as glad as we are," said the delivery men.